GROLIER
B O O K S

DISNEP's

THE LITTLE MERMAID

and Spot

One fine ocean morning the Little Mermaid and her friends were playing ball.

"Catch, Spot," Ariel called. She threw the ball as hard as she could.

"It really went a long way that time," said Flounder. The little yellow fish was Ariel's best friend.

But Ariel's other friend, Spot, didn't mind. The baby whale happily chased after the ball.

The ball landed near a sunken ship.
"Watch out, Spot!" Ariel shouted.
But the baby whale couldn't stop.
CRASH! Spot bumped into the ship.
He wasn't hurt, and he kept chasing the ball.

Flounder looked at the
large hole the whale had made in the ship.
"Maybe Spot is getting too big to play ball," he said.
Ariel watched her friend trying to pick up the tiny ball.
"Spot's not too big. The ball is too small," she answered.

Ariel took the ball
to her father,
King Triton.

"This ball is too small for Spot," Ariel said.
"Could you make it bigger, please?"

"Of course, Ariel," her father replied.
He aimed his trident at Spot's ball.
ZAP! The small ball became a big ball.
"That's perfect," Ariel said. "Thank you."

"Come on, Spot, let's play," the young mermaid called. She threw the ball again.

But Ariel didn't see a very small crab named Crabby. He was taking his morning walk.

Crabby was a very grumpy crab.

Ariel thought he was grumpy because he had no friends.

Flounder thought he had no friends because he was grumpy.

Either way, Crabby was also very unlucky that morning.

BONK! The big ball landed right on Crabby's small head.

"Oh, dear!" Ariel cried. "I'm very sorry, Crabby. I didn't see you there. Are you hurt?"

"You did that
on purpose!"
Crabby shrieked.
"You're picking on
me because you're
bigger than I am."
   "No, I'm not,"
Ariel said. "It was
an accident. I really
am sorry."

But the angry little crab didn't believe her.

Ariel felt terrible, but there was nothing more she could do.

Soon afterward the friends began to play ball again. CRASH! This time Spot swam into King Triton. "Oooff!" the king gasped in surprise.

"Spot!" the king shouted at the baby whale. "You made me drop my trident!"

Triton was so angry that he didn't notice what his trident was doing.

ZAP! Something small became something big.

Spot went to retrieve the king's trident.

"That whale is too big to play ball!" King Triton told Ariel. "I could . . . I mean, someone could get hurt!"

"But, Father, he's just a baby," said Ariel. "He'll learn to be more careful!"

But Triton was still angry. When Spot
returned, the king said, "Spot, you're no longer
allowed to play ball!"

Poor Spot. He swam away in tears.

None of them noticed that they were being watched.

That afternoon
Ariel went looking
for Spot.

"Spot, where
are you?"
she called.

The mermaid
called and
called, but she
couldn't find
her friend.

Ariel swam past the hole in the sunken ship. Suddenly a giant claw reached out and grabbed her by the arm!

"Stop! Let me go! Help!" she shouted. But no one heard her as she was pulled into the ship!

Meanwhile,
Flounder was
looking for Ariel.
She had promised
to meet him,
but she wasn't
in her room.

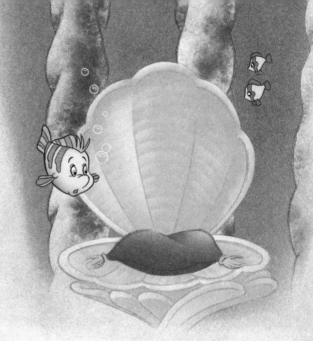

"Arrrielll!" Flounder called. "Where are you?"

As Flounder swam past the sunken ship, he thought he heard Ariel's voice.

"Ariel," he whispered, "are you in there?"

The little fish peered inside the ship.

Flounder couldn't believe his eyes. "It's a monster!" he gasped. "And it's got Ariel locked up in a cage!"

"Bounce a ball off my head!" the huge monster roared at Ariel. "Now you know how it feels to be bullied by someone bigger than you!"

"Crabby," said Ariel, "it really was an accident. I would *never* hurt someone who is smaller than I am." But the nasty crab wouldn't let her go. "Now that *I'm* big, I can pick on anyone who's smaller than I am," he snapped.

That made
Ariel angry.
"That's not right,
Crabby!"
she answered.
"Now let me
out of here."
"Never!"
Crabby jeered.

Flounder had seen enough. He quickly went
to get King Triton.

Flounder found the king talking to Sebastian.
"Your Majesty!" Flounder cried. "Crabby has
grown into a big monster. And he's captured Ariel!"

King Triton and Sebastian followed Flounder
to the sunken ship.

"Release my daughter at once!" thundered
King Triton. "Or I'll teach you a lesson you'll
never forget."

"You heard the king!" Sebastian added from
behind Triton.

The king swam closer to the hole in the
sunken ship.

Suddenly a giant claw shot out and grabbed
Triton's arm.

The king was so surprised he dropped his trident.

The giant crab quickly grabbed the magic trident. He pointed it at the king and laughed.

"So you'd like to teach me a lesson?" Crabby asked the king. "Well, maybe I'll teach you a lesson instead!"

The crab pointed
the trident at the king.

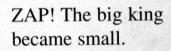

ZAP! The big king
became small.

In fact, Triton
was as small
as Sebastian.

Luckily, Triton and Sebastian were able to hide beneath some seaweed so Crabby couldn't find them.

Crabby didn't see Flounder swim into the ship. The little fish told Ariel what had happened.

Ariel was furious!

"Flounder, we need help," she said. "Big help. Tell my father to find Spot. He'll know just what to do."

Flounder gave King Triton and Sebastian the
message. Together they went to look for Spot.
"There he is, Your Majesty!" Sebastian cried.
When Spot saw the king, he tried to swim away.

He thought King Triton was still angry with him.
"Wait!" Triton called. "Ariel needs you and
so do I. Will you help us?"
Of course, Spot was happy to help his friends.

Together they raced back to the ship.
"There he is, Spot!" bellowed King
Triton. He pointed at Crabby.
The giant crab just laughed at Spot.
"Another big shot who
wants to be cut down
to size," he said.

Crabby aimed the magic trident at the baby whale. ZAP!

But Spot was too fast. Crabby missed him.

Spot quickly grabbed the ship's anchor and chain from the ocean floor.

The whale swam
around and around
the giant crab.

Crabby got tangled
in the chain.
"Help! Stop!
What's happening?"
he shouted.

Soon Spot had Crabby tied in a knot.
The big crab dropped the trident!

While Flounder went to free Ariel, Spot picked up the trident. He pointed it at the king.

"Now, remember, Spot," said Triton. "Think big—but not *too* big."

ZAP! The small king became a big king again.

When Ariel swam out of the ship, she was happy to see her father thanking Spot.

"You know, Ariel," her father said. "This fellow is just the right size for a baby whale."

"Does that mean he can play ball with us?" Ariel asked.

"Whenever he wants to," King Triton replied.

"But someone here is *not* the right size," declared Triton. "Being big doesn't make you a monster, Crabby. But picking on others does."

Triton pointed his trident at Crabby. "I'm going to make sure he can't pick on anyone ever again," he told Ariel.

ZAP! The big crab became a small crab.

Ariel gave the baby whale a kiss on the
cheek. "You're a big hero," she told Spot. "Not
because you're a big whale, but because you have a
big heart."

And as for Crabby . . . well, he was still the crabbiest crab in the ocean. But he learned that you don't make friends by picking on others. You make friends by being bighearted.